❧ BOOK REVIEW

Caldone's line-and-watercolor illustrations have all the verve and good humor associated with his work, and the varied and irresistible rhythm of the verses carries the nonsense along at a good pace, enhancing its appeal to the very young.

from THE BOOKLIST

This book is a presentation of Weekly Reader Books. Weekly Reader Books offers book clubs for children from preschool through high school. For further information write to: **Weekly Reader Books,** 4343 Equity Drive, Columbus, Ohio 43228.

A Clarion Book. Reprinted with the permission of Houghton Mifflin Company.

Clarion Books / Ticknor & Fields, a Houghton Mifflin Company
Copyright © 1985 by Paul Galdone

Library of Congress Cataloging in Publication Data
Galdone, Paul.
    Cat goes fiddle-i-fee.
    Summary: An old English rhyme names all the animals a farm boy feeds on his daily rounds.
    1. Nursery rhymes, English.   2.Children's poetry, English. [1. Nursery rhymes.   2. English poetry]   1. Title.
PZ8.3.G1218Cat   1985   398′.8   85-2686   ISBN 0-89919-336-6

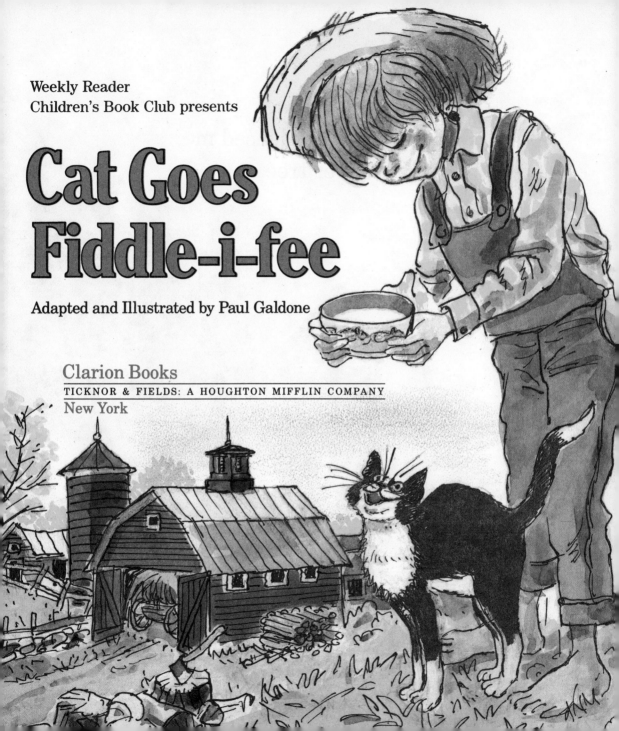

Cat Goes Fiddle-i-fee

Adapted and Illustrated by Paul Galdone

Clarion Books
TICKNOR & FIELDS: A HOUGHTON MIFFLIN COMPANY
New York

I had a cat and the cat pleased me,
I fed my cat by yonder tree.

Cat goes fiddle-i-fee.

I had a hen and the hen pleased me,
I fed my hen by yonder tree.

Hen goes chimmy-chuck, chimmy-chuck,
Cat goes fiddle-i-fee.

I had a duck and the duck pleased me,
I fed my duck by yonder tree.

Duck goes quack, quack,
Hen goes chimmy-chuck, chimmy-chuck,
Cat goes fiddle-i-fee.

I had a goose and the goose pleased me,
I fed my goose by yonder tree.

Goose goes swishy, swashy,
Duck goes quack, quack,
Hen goes chimmy-chuck, chimmy-chuck,
Cat goes fiddle-i-fee.

I had a sheep and the sheep pleased me,
I fed my sheep by yonder tree.

Sheep goes baa, baa,
Goose goes swishy, swashy,
Duck goes quack, quack,
Hen goes chimmy-chuck, chimmy-chuck,
Cat goes fiddle-i-fee.

I had a pig and the pig pleased me,
I fed my pig by yonder tree.

Pig goes griffy, gruffy,
Sheep goes baa, baa,
Goose goes swishy, swashy,
Duck goes quack, quack,
Hen goes chimmy-chuck, chimmy-chuck,
Cat goes fiddle-i-fee.

I had a cow and the cow pleased me,
I fed my cow by yonder tree.

Cow goes moo, moo,
Pig goes griffy, gruffy,
Sheep goes baa, baa,
Goose goes swishy, swashy,
Duck goes quack, quack,
Hen goes chimmy-chuck, chimmy-chuck,
Cat goes fiddle-i-fee.

I had a horse and the horse pleased me,
I fed my horse by yonder tree.

Horse goes neigh, neigh,
Cow goes moo, moo,
Pig goes griffy, gruffy,
Sheep goes baa, baa,
Goose goes swishy, swashy,
Duck goes quack, quack,
Hen goes chimmy-chuck, chimmy-chuck,
Cat goes fiddle-i-fee.

I had a dog and the dog pleased me,
I fed my dog by yonder tree.

Dog goes bow-wow, bow-wow,
Horse goes neigh, neigh,
Cow goes moo, moo,
Pig goes griffy, gruffy,
Sheep goes baa, baa,
Goose goes swishy, swashy,
Duck goes quack, quack,
Hen goes chimmy-chuck, chimmy-chuck,
Cat goes fiddle-i-fee.

Then Grandma came
and she fed me...

while the others dozed
by yonder tree.

And cat went fiddle-i-fee.